This

Harry

book belongs to

....

SCELIDOSAURUS
(ske-LI-doh-SAW-rus)

TYRANNOSAURUS
(tie-RAN-oh-SAW-rus)

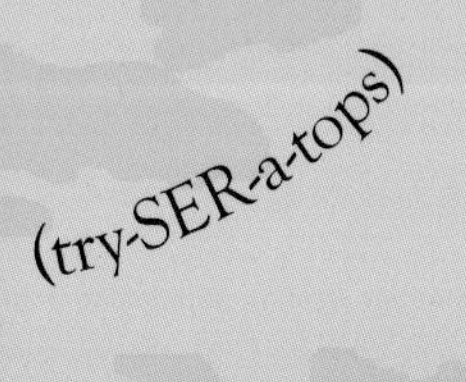

TRICERATOPS
(try-SER-a-tops)

PTERODACTYL
(TER-oh-DAC-til)

STEGOSAURUS
(STEG-oh-SAW-rus)

APATOSAURUS
(a-PAT-oh-SAW-rus)

ANCHISAURUS
(AN-ki-SAW-rus)

SCELIDOSAURUS
(ske-LI-doh-SAW-rus)

TYRANNOSAURUS
(tie-RAN-oh-SAW-rus)

TRICERATOPS
(try-SER-a-tops)

PTERODACTYL
(TER-oh-DAC-til)

STEGOSAURUS
(STEG-oh-SAW-rus)

APATOSAURUS
(a-PAT-oh-SAW-rus)

ANCHISAURUS
(AN-ki-SAW-rus)

Three Raaaahs for Cosmo, Albie and Circe,
the wee Millers of Holmeknowe! – I.W.

For Luciana Olivia Linciano – A.R.

PUFFIN BOOKS
Published by the Penguin Group: London, New York, Australia, Canada, India, Ireland, New Zealand and South Africa
Penguin Books Ltd, Registered Offices: 80 Strand, London WC2R 0RL, England

puffinbooks.com

First published 2007
Published in this edition 2008

3 5 7 9 10 8 6 4 2

Made and printed in China
ISBN: 978–1–856–13239–8

Harry and the Dinosaurs make a Splash

Ian Whybrow and Adrian Reynolds

PUFFIN

Harry and the dinosaurs loved the wave pool at the indoor Water World. Jumping over the waves with Sam was FUN!

Then a big wave came and knocked them all over! That spoiled it! That wasn't nice at all. The water made them cough and got in their eyes.

"Raaah!" said Anchisaurus. "This tastes terrible, Harry!"

"Raaah!" said Triceratops. "Our bath at home is much nicer!"

"Quick," said Scelidosaurus. "Let's run away!"

So Harry and the dinosaurs ran back to Nan.
"Why don't you come in this pool?" she said, but they didn't want to.
"Raaah! We hate water now," said Tyrannosaurus.

Nan said, "What a shame them old waves spoiled things for you. Let's see if something cool will help."

She took them for some juice and double scoops of ice cream with extra sticky stuff. Ahhh! That helped a lot!

"Are you ready to go swimming again now, Harry?" asked Nan.

Harry wasn't sure. "My dinosaurs don't like getting splashed," he said. "But maybe they'll go in if you come too, Nan."

Nan looked worried.

"I'm ever so sorry," she said. "I haven't been swimming for years. I expect I should sink like a stone!"

Sam said it was stupid coming all this way and then being too scared to go in.

That was why Nan threw a bucket of water over her.

"Mind your own business, Miss Cleverstick!" she shouted.

Harry took Nan to settle down.

"You're not allowed to splash people in swimming pools, Nan!" he told her.

Nan said quite right, shocking, she was ashamed of herself.

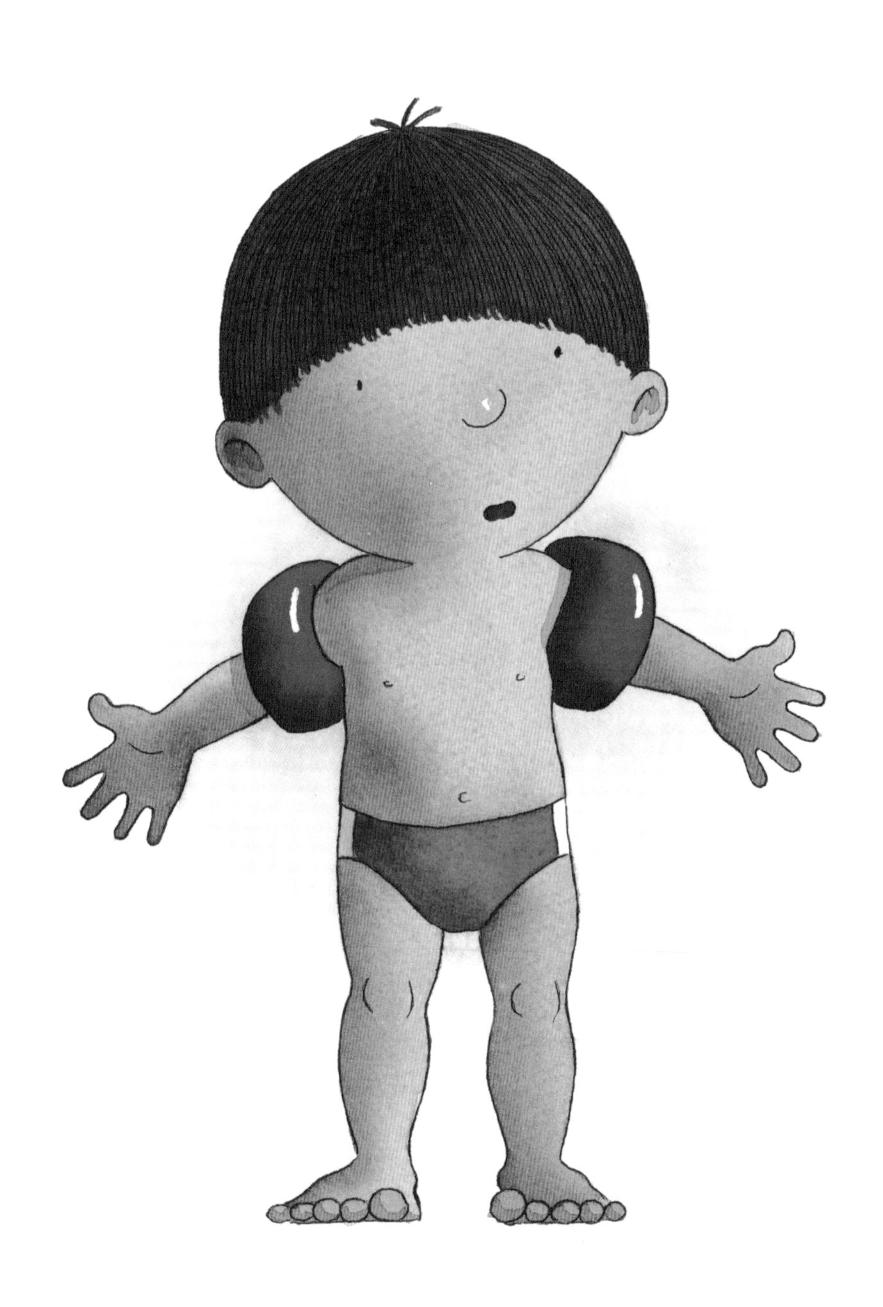

So Harry and the dinosaurs took her to watch the people on the water slide.

Nan thought that looked tree-mendous!

"Why don't you try that, Harry?" she said. "Sam would take you, I'm sure."

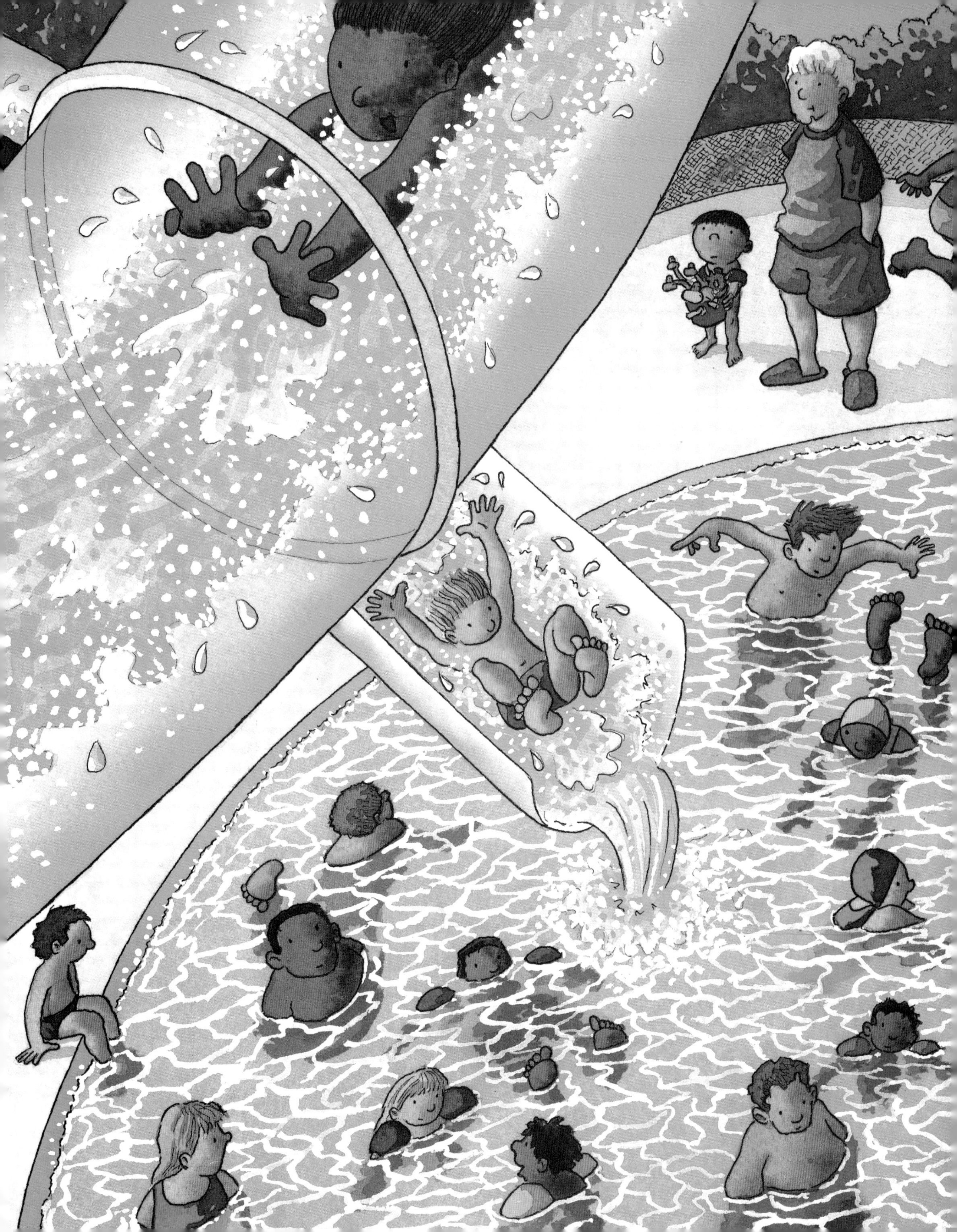

It *did* look really fun, but Harry and the dinosaurs didn't feel *quite* brave enough yet.

"Raaah!" said Apatosaurus. "We don't want to go with Sam!"

"We only want to go with you, Nan," said Harry.

"That's ever so high . . ." said Nan. "But I suppose we'll be all right if we stick together!"

She grabbed Harry’s hand and they rushed off to the shop. Nan chose a bright yellow swimsuit for herself and some goggles for Harry.

“Here, pop these on,” said Nan, “while I buy myself some senior armbands.”

"Let's go!" said the dinosaurs. "If Nan can do it, we can do it!"

They climbed right up to the top and they were only a little bit scared.

RAAAAHH!

What a surprise for Sam!
Nan and Harry and the dinosaurs
made the biggest SPLASH of the day!

"Cool!" laughed Sam. "And I thought you
you were scared of the water."
"I was nervous, that's all," said Nan.
"But Harry's helping me."
"And my dinosaurs!" said Harry.
"They're helping too!"

“Raaah!” said Pterodactyl. “I’m a dive bomber!”
“We like rough waves now,” said Scelidosaurus. “Look, we can bite them!”

"How do I look?" laughed Nan. "Am I sinking like a stone?"

"No, you're definitely swimming!" said Harry and the dinosaurs. "You look tree-mendous!"

ENDOSAURUS

SCELIDOSAURUS

(ske-LI-doh-SAW-rus)

TYRANNOSAURUS

(tie-RAN-oh-SAW-rus)

TRICERATOPS

(try-SER-a-tops)

STEGOSAURUS

(STEG-oh-SAW-rus)

PTERODACTYL

(TER-oh-DAC-til)

APATOSAURUS

(a-PAT-oh-SAW-rus)

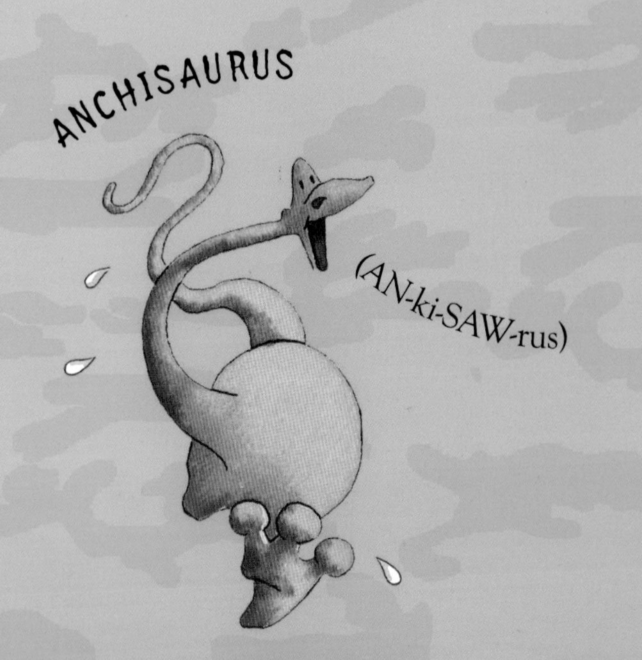

ANCHISAURUS

(AN-ki-SAW-rus)

PTERODACTYL

(TER-oh-DAC-til)

ANCHISAURUS

(AN-ki-SAW-rus)